This Nature Storybook belongs to:

Evan

Thank you for being a great
part of the Elephant group
2017 – 2018

WALKER BOOKS

From everyone in the
Jungle Room.

About the author

Vivian French lives in Bristol, in the
south-west of England. Every spring when her
daughters were little they visited the pond next door
to collect some frogspawn, bring it home,
and watch the tadpoles hatch.
Her cat was always VERY interested.
Now that her children are grown up, Vivian
travels about, telling stories and writing books.
"A Song for Little Toad" was shortlisted
for the Smarties Book Prize.

About the illustrator

Alison Bartlett also lives in Bristol,
with her son Joel and two Jack Russell terriers.
She has illustrated several books by Vivian French,
including "Oliver's Vegetables", which was recommended
for the National Art Library Illustration Awards.
Before she painted the pictures for this book
Alison thought frogspawn was "disgusting" —
now she thinks it's amazing.

For Jane Slade
V.F.

For Rebecca, with much love
A.B.

Consultant: Martin Jenkins

First published 2000 by Walker Books Ltd
87 Vauxhall Walk, London SE11 5HJ

This edition published 2015

4 6 8 10 9 7 5 3

Text © 2000 Vivian French

Illustrations © 2000 Alison Bartlett

This book has been typeset in Tapioca

Printed in China

British Library Cataloguing in Publication Data:
a catalogue record for this book is available from the British Library.

ISBN 978-1-4063-6465-1

www.walker.co.uk

Growing
Frogs

Vivian French   illustrated by Alison Bartlett

WALKER BOOKS
AND SUBSIDIARIES
LONDON · BOSTON · SYDNEY · AUCKLAND

Once, when I was little, my mum read me a story about a frog that drank and drank and drank, and grew **bigger** and **bigger** and **bigger**.

Afterwards Mum asked me if I'd like to watch some real frogs growing.

"I know where there's a pond with lots of frogs' eggs in it," she said. "We could bring some home."

I was frightened. "I don't want any frogs jumping about getting **bigger** and **bigger** and **bigger**," I said.

But Mum gave me a hug. "It's only a story," she said. "Even when our frogs are grown up they'll still be smaller than my hand."

"Oh," I said. "OK."

Next day we went
to look at the pond.
The water was dark
brown, and there
was grey jelly stuff
floating on the top.

"Yuck!" I said.

"There's the frogspawn," said Mum.
And she pointed to the grey jelly stuff.
"I bet that was laid last Friday night.
The frogs were croaking so loudly,
I couldn't get to sleep."

Male frogs croak to attract female frogs
for mating. The females lay eggs called frogspawn.

"You see the black dot in the middle of each jelly shell?" said Mum. "That's going to grow into a tadpole."

"Where are the frogs?" I asked.
"Tadpoles grow into frogs," she said.
"Little ones — no giant frogs here!"

10

Mum put some pondweed
and some stones into a bag.
She filled a bucket with
pond water, then I scooped
a *little* of the frogspawn
into it.

Always use pond water for growing frogs at home.
Tap water has chemicals like fluoride in it,
which might poison them.

When we got home we put everything into a big fish tank in the kitchen.

The cat kept peering at it, so we had to put a wire net over the top.

I counted
twenty-seven
little black dots.
Each dot was inside
its own jelly shell.

The tank needs to be somewhere that's cool and away from direct sunlight.

13

Every day when I woke up
I went straight downstairs
to look at the frogspawn.

The little dots
grew into bigger dots,

and then into
tiny commas.

In a tank, the eggs hatch into tadpoles about ten days after they are laid.

And one morning
I saw the first tadpole
wriggling out of its
jelly shell!

At first the tadpoles didn't do much.
They just stayed close to their jelly shells
and nibbled at the pondweed.

But after two or three days
they looked quite different. There
were feathery things on their heads
and I could see their eyes.

The feathery bits are called gills and they're
what underwater animals use for breathing.

They swam **very** fast.

Ten of the eggs
didn't hatch out.
The black dots went
dull and cloudy,
and Mum took
them away.

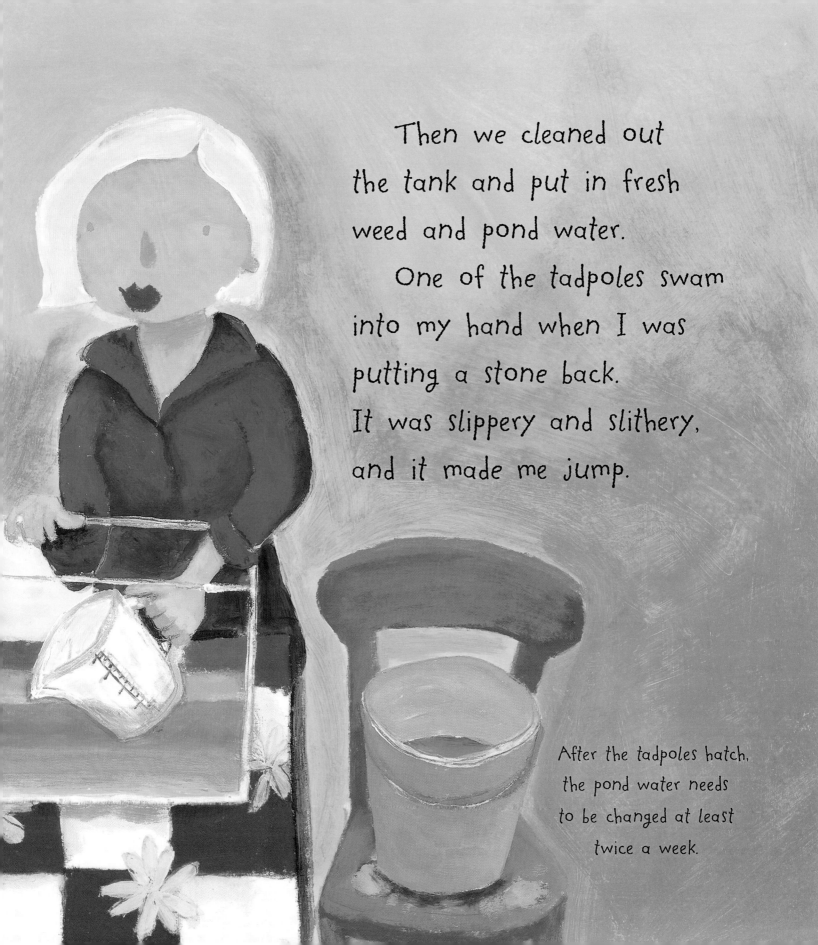

Then we cleaned out
the tank and put in fresh
weed and pond water.
One of the tadpoles swam
into my hand when I was
putting a stone back.
It was slippery and slithery,
and it made me jump.

After the tadpoles hatch,
the pond water needs
to be changed at least
twice a week.

After a bit I got used to having tadpoles and I didn't look at them so often.

When Mum told me their little feathery bits had gone I didn't believe her.

But it was **true.**

Tadpoles only have gills outside their bodies at first.
Then they grow gills inside their bodies
and the outside ones disappear.

It was me that saw the next change, though.

"Look!"

I shouted, and Mum rushed to see.
Some of the tadpoles had grown two
little bumps. Mum said the bumps
would grow into back legs.

They grew very quickly.

One day there were
two little bumps.

The next day the
bumps were stumps.

22

The day after that they were almost proper legs.

And when the feet unfolded they were webbed, like tiny browny-green fans.

"They aren't tadpoles any more," I said.
"They're not-quite-frogs."

The not-quite-frogs grew front legs next.

And then their tails got shorter

and their mouths got **wider**.

"Now they're frogs," Mum said.
"Baby ones."

Soon the baby frogs were popping up and gulping at the surface of the water.

One of them tried to climb on to the stones, but it slid off. Mum said they were getting ready to leave the water.

"Grown-up frogs breathe air," she said. "That's what the stones are for — so our frogs can climb out of the water and breathe."

As tadpoles slowly turn into frogs, they grow lungs for breathing air and their gills disappear.

Not long after that Mum said it was
time to take our baby frogs back to live
in the pond with all the other baby frogs.

I was sorry to leave them, but Mum
said we could come back and visit
every day.

Baby frogs need space to grow and room to hop around.
Grown-up frogs live most of their lives on land,
only returning to their ponds to breed.

One rainy morning a week later
Mum woke me up very early.
"Hurry!" she said, and we ran downstairs
and out to the pond.

There were hundreds of tiny
frogs hopping over the grass.

"They're looking for dark wet places to
live in," Mum said. "But they won't go far,
and in a couple of years they'll be back
to lay frogspawn of their own."

"Will they be bigger then?" I asked.

"Just a little," said Mum.

"Good," I said. "I like
having frogs jumping about
getting bigger
and bigger
and bigger!"

Index

Look up the pages to find out about
all these froggy things.
Don't forget to look at both kinds of word –
this kind and *this* kind.

Frogs are in danger – please help!

Rules for frog-lovers

- ⊙ Don't ever take frogspawn from a wild pond.

- ⊙ If you take frogspawn from a garden pond, only take a LITTLE.

- ⊙ Always take your frogs back to the pond they came from.

Note to Parents

Sharing books with children is one of the best ways to help them learn. And it's one of the best ways they learn to read, too.

Nature Storybooks are beautifully illustrated, award-winning information picture books whose focus on animals has a strong appeal for children. They can be read as stories, revisited and enjoyed again and again, inviting children to become excited about a subject, to think and discover, and to want to find out more.

Each book is an adventure into the real world that broadens children's experience and develops their curiosity and understanding – and that's the best kind of learning there is.

Note to Teachers

Nature Storybooks provide memorable reading experiences for children in Key Stages 1 and 2 (Years 1–4), and also offer many learning opportunities for exploring a topic through words and pictures.

By working with the stories, either individually or together, children can respond to the animal world through a variety of activities, including drawing and painting, role play, talking and writing.

The books provide a rich starting-point for further research and for developing children's knowledge of information genres.

Nature Storybooks support the literacy curriculum in a variety of ways, providing:
- a focus for a whole class topic
- high-quality texts for guided reading
- a resource for the class read-aloud programme
- information texts for the class and school library for developing children's individual reading interests

Find more information on how to use Nature Storybooks in the classroom at
www.walker.co.uk/naturestorybooks
Nature Storybooks support KS 1–2 English and KS 1–2 Science